PuP
The Sea Otter

Written by

Jonathan London

Illustrated by

Sean London

WESTWINDS
PRESS®

On the first day of spring,
off the coast of California,
the sun bursts out from behind
a cloud . . .

~and a baby sea otter is born!

Pup the Sea Otter—

a fluffy ball of fur
with eyes open
and teeth already showing—
nuzzles his mother's belly.

Full and dreamy
with Mother's milk,
Pup the Sea Otter *yaaawns*
and sleeps on Mama's chest.

She grooms him
    with her paws and teeth and tongue,
licking his fluffy fur and slippery flippers—

slurp slurp slurp

until she, too, falls asleep,
    hugging him close,
wrapped in seaweed.

*B*ut Pup is hungry,
    and his hunger wakes them up.
Now Mama must eat for both of them.

Wrapped in kelp
    (so he doesn't drift away),
Pup the Sea Otter
    bobs like a fuzzy cork . . .

while Mama dives
and forages for food
on the sea bottom.

Pup squeals and cries—

Eeeeeeee!

Mama! Where is Mama?

There she is!

She pops up with a tasty crab
      tucked in a pocket under her front leg!
Then she rolls on her back and—

munch   crunch   munch!

(shell and all)!

ow she dives for more . . .
down and down
to the ocean floor . . .
and rises with a large abalone.

This time, she rolls on her back,
pulls a big rock from the pocket
under her forearm, and . . .

Whack! Whack! Whack!

She cracks open the hard shell—

munch

crunch

munch!

After she eats, Mama holds her little one
   on her belly again,
so Pup the Sea Otter
   can nuzzle and nurse.

Sometimes alone,
    sometimes in a raft
of other mothers and pups
    floating in the sea—

they sway with the swells,
    swirl and sleep.
She grooms and dives for prey,
    as the days grow into weeks.

At one month old
     Pup the Sea Otter
eats solid food for the first time!
     His mother brings him
shelled oysters and bits of abalone.
     But he wants to dive with his mother.

At first, he's a weak swimmer—
     he's too buoyant
and pops back up like a rubber duck!
     But he learns from her . . .

and at three months old
    it happens!
He sheds his fluffy pup coat
    and his heavy adult fur grows in.

Now he can dive like his mother!

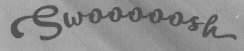

Down and down, trailing bubbles
    through the kelp forest,
powered by his strong hind limbs.

And his catlike paws
    and sensitive whiskers
lead him to his prey.

There!

Clusters of small clams!

Pup pulls them one by one
from the billowing mud,
tucks them into his
armpit pocket . . .

and races Mama to the surface.
   AIR!
He rolls over and pops one in his mouth—
   munch crunch munch.

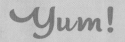

When his belly is full,
      it's time to rest, and groom,
and float, and sleep.
And when he wakes . . .

it's time to play with the other pups!

To race and chase

and swish and tumble.

To swirl and twist

and rock and roll!

Suddenly, the other pups are gone.
     Pup the Sea Otter is all alone.
He hears waves crashing.

Something is coming.

A fin!

Slicing through the water
right toward him.

Pup squeals and cries—

Eeeeeeee!

Mama! Where is Mama?

There she is!

She grabs Pup by the scruff of his neck,
    and dives down and down.
Just as the Great White Shark
    is nearly to them . . .

Swish!

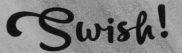

Mama slides through a narrow crack . . .
and pops up on the other side—

Pup is safe!

Summer comes and summer goes.
The swells roll in and waves crash.
And Pup the Sea Otter grows and grows.

By eight months old,
   he's learned all he needs to know
from his mother.

   One day he's living side by side with her . . .
      and the next . . .
he's with a raft of young males!

Tumbling and rolling,
   racing and wrestling,
eating and grooming,
   and resting, wrapped in kelp.

At home in the sea.

Author's Note

Sea otters are one of the most important animals living in the coastal seas of the North Pacific. Among their favorite foods are sea urchins, which live in the kelp forests along the shore. Sea urchins eat kelp. So sea otters help save the kelp by eating the urchins. And kelp is extremely important to coastal sea life.

Weighing up to ninety-nine pounds, sea otters are the largest member of the weasel family, which includes weasels, skunks, badgers, and wolverines. But they're small compared to other sea mammals, like whales, dolphins, porpoises, sea lions, seals, and walruses.

Besides sea urchins, sea otters love to eat clams, crabs, mussels, abalone, and oysters, putting them in direct competition with commercial fisheries. But remember, sea otters help save kelp, and kelp is important to the shellfish that fishermen depend upon.

Luckily for fishermen, sea otter mothers usually only give birth to one pup per pregnancy. The pup in this story is a Southern—or California—sea otter. Northern sea otters live off the coasts of Alaska, British Columbia, and Washington.

Sea otters are fascinating. They have the thickest fur of any animal—from 200,000 to over a million hairs per square inch! Unlike other sea mammals, they have very little blubber. Instead, sea otters depend on their dense fur for warmth. Sea otters rarely climb out of the sea. They spend much of their day diving for food, eating, and grooming, which is necessary for their fur to keep its warmth. Like humans, sea otters use tools—rocks for breaking shells. Sea otters have to eat more than a third of their weight in food every day. Imagine a child weighing sixty pounds eating more than twenty pounds of food per day!

When they forage for food, sea otters can hold their breath as long as five minutes and dive down over 300 feet. They are strong and graceful swimmers.

Prior to hunting there were hundreds of thousands of sea otters in the North Pacific. But between 1741 and 1911, most were killed for their fur. The population plummeted to just a few thousand otters. In 1911, hunting was prohibited, and in 1977 the California sea otter became protected by the Endangered Species Act. Since then, the California sea otter population has increased to around 3,000.

Even so, today their numbers are going down, and nearly one-half of all sea otter pups die each year. Some die from great white shark attacks, but *most* die from pollution of the coastal waters. The biggest threat to sea otters is oil spills.

Thanks to education and conservation efforts, the world's cutest furry animal just might stand a chance of surviving. *Long live Pup the Sea Otter!*

For Sean, Steph, Leah, sweet Maureen, and Doug P.
—Jonathan London

For Mom, Dad, Stephanie, and all the sea otters.
—Sean London

Library of Congress Cataloging-in-Publication Data

Names: London, Jonathan, 1947- author. | London, Sean, illustrator.
Title: Pup the Sea Otter / written by Jonathan London ; illustrations by Sean London.
Description: Portland, Oregon : WestWinds Press, [2017] | Summary: The first year of life for a male sea otter, as his mother tenderly cares for him and teaches him how to survive on his own.
Identifiers: LCCN 2016034581 (print) | LCCN 2016058631 (ebook) | ISBN 9781943328871 (pbk.) | ISBN 9781943328888 ()
Subjects: LCSH: Sea otter--Juvenile fiction. | CYAC: Sea otter--Fiction. | Otters--Fiction. Classification: LCC PZ10.3.L8534 Pu 2017 (print) | LCC PZ10.3.L8534 (ebook) | DDC [E]--dc23
LC record available at https://lccn.loc.gov/2016034581

Editor: Michelle McCann
Designer: Vicki Knapton

Published by WestWinds Press®
An imprint of

GRAPHIC ARTS
BOOKS®

P.O. Box 56118
Portland, Oregon 97238-6118
www.graphicartsbooks.com

Printed in China